I0788397

17 STROKES:
A BRUSHSTROKE OF THE SOUL

BY DEBORAH S. MCINTOSH

ALL OF THE WRITINGS AND PAINTINGS CONTAINED HEREIN ARE MY OWN CREATIONS.

DEBORAH S. MCINTOSH

SEPTEMBER 24TH, 2025

———————————————————

LIFE GRANTS US WONDER
IN THE SPLENDOR OF THE DAY
LET'S CELEBRATE

———————————————————

PUPPETS ON THE STAGE
SWAYING TO THE MUSIC'S BEAT
WHO IS PULLING STRINGS?

SERENE AND PEACEFUL REFLECTIONS OF TODAY WE SHARED TOGETHER

CARROT DANGLED BAIT HOOKED INTO ANOTHER SPACE AND TIME TODAY

NO MATTER WHAT'S THROWN, I CAN STILL SEE MY WAY THROUGH THE MIRE AND THE MUCK

CONTEMPLATING MANKIND, WAS IT WORTH THE SACRIFICE JESUS MADE THAT DAY?

DAY CHANGES TO NIGHT
AND A RAINBOW CIRCLED MOON
BRIGHTENS UP THE SKY

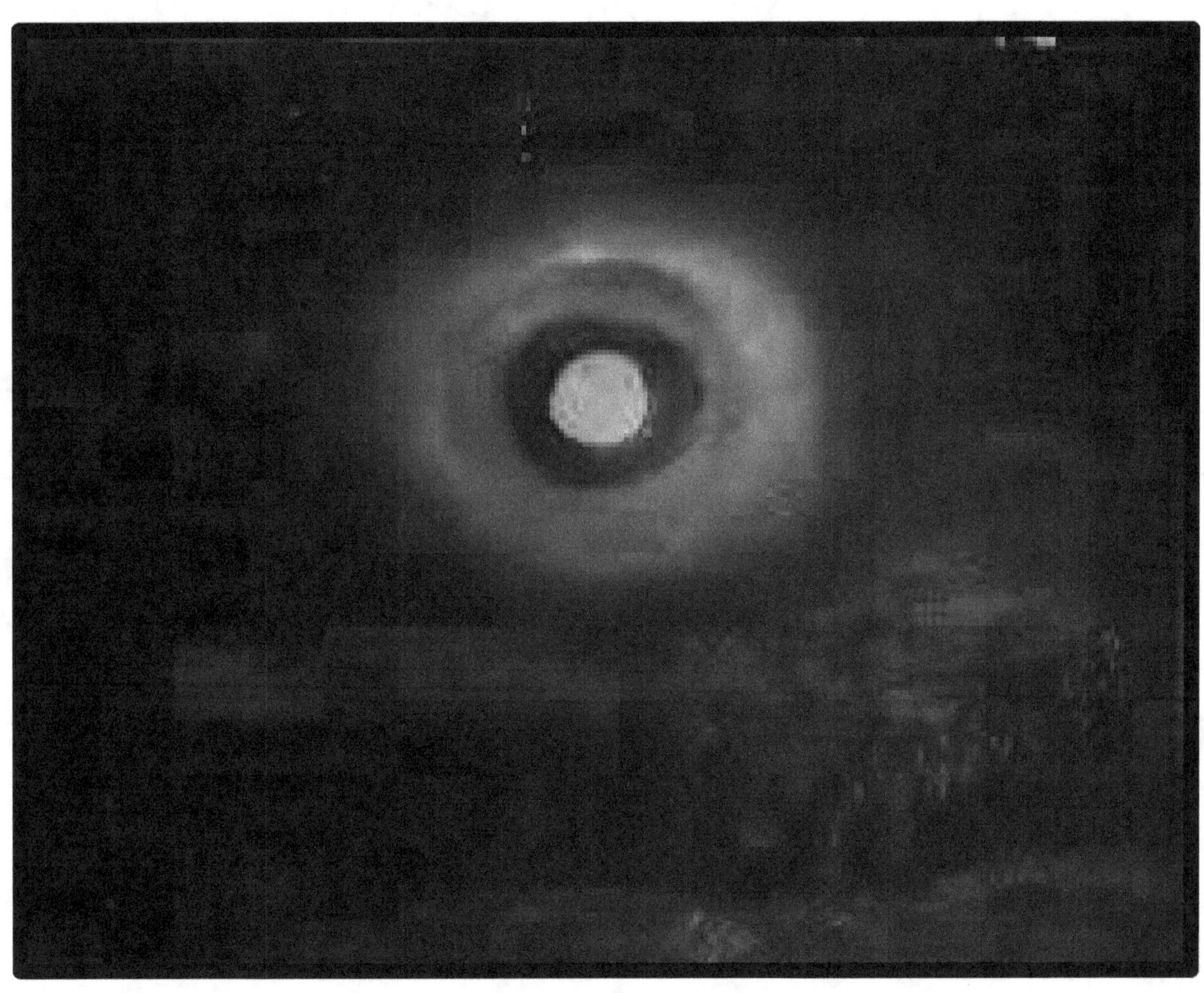

RACING FOR THE DAWN
OF A BRIGHT NEW DAY
BRACING FOR THE STORM

━·━

IN THE PRISM OF MIND
FRACTURED IN MANY PLACES
AN ANGEL STANDS GUARD

━·━

IN THE DISTANT CITY
VERDANT GREENS LAY TO SLUMBER
UNDER MOONLIGHT'S GLOW

BEHIND MASKS WE WATCH
WAITING FOR THE TIME TO POUNCE
UNSUSPECTINGLY

TIME STANDS STILL, TICK TOCK
ANTICIPATION BREAKS FREE
MIDNIGHT LOVERS WAIT

**SHADOWS OF THE PAST
BREAK FREE INTO THE PRESENT
CANVAS OF MY MIND**

I WATCH, WAIT AND SEE
SAYING NOTHING, LOST IN THOUGHT
TILL THE TIME IS RIGHT

HIDDEN IN THE DEPTHS
HER HEART BORE THE BRUNT OF GRIEF
UNTOLD UNTIL DEATH

SPLASHES OF COLOR
BRIGHTEN NATURE'S VAST ARRAY
OF LIFE STRUGGLING FREE

IN THIS HEART OF STONE
CAPTURED BY THE BOUNDARIES
TWO SOULS PLUNGE THE DEEP

FRACTAL DISPLACEMENT
SYNAPSES FIRE THROUGH MY MIND
JUMBLING EVERYTHING

MULTI-COLORED SKY
SETS THE SCENE IN WINTERTIME
AT DAY'S TIME TO REST

THE MIND'S CREATION
SOMETIMES IS A JUMBLED MESS
EXPLODING COLORS

A LIMB EXTENDED
PERFECT PERCH TO OVERSEE
GOD'S WHOLE CREATION

CHILDREN RUN TO PLAY
ON THE WINGS OF PEGASUS
LAUGHTER'S ECHO HEARD

IN THE CIRCLE BUILT
AN OFFERING OF RED ROSES
TIME TO FACE THE DAY

UNEXPLORED DEPTHS
HIDDEN DIMENSIONS OF ME
IN THE DEEP BLUE SEA

PETAL BY PETAL
I PLUCK ONLY TO FIND OUT
JUST A STEM REMAINS

IMAGINATIONS' UNPARALLELED FLOWERS SEED THE ARTISTS' MIND

EVERY COLOR
FRAILTY BUILT WITHIN ITS SKIN
EXPOSES MADNESS

STRATOSPHERIC WINDS
HOLD THE ANGELS HIGH ABOVE
WHO DO WATCH AND WAIT

ANCIENT DAYS LONG AGO
ON THE SHORES OF SACRIFICE
THEREIN CHANGE BEGAN

WE CHANGED COURSE MIDSTREAM
STOMP INSTEAD OF PIROUETTE
SQUARE DANCERS WE WERE

MUDDIED WATERS FLOW
THROUGH FIELDS OF GREEN AND AMBER
TO SETTLE ON THE SHORE

ENGLAND'S ROLLING HILLS
GAVE RISE TO A BRAND NEW WORLD
FAR ACROSS THE SEA

HARDENED OVER TIME
PATHS WE PACED WORN SMOOTH
FROM USE
EMERGE FROM THE ROCK

PLEASURE FLOATS ON HIGHS
TRANSCENDING DREARY PROBLEMS
'TIS AN OPIATE

LABYRINTH OF MIND
SERENE BLUE GREEN GRASSY FIELDS
TRANQUIL IN NATURE

SHADOW'S DEEPEST REALM MASKS SELF SHROUDED BY THE VEIL OF SELF, WHO AM I?

NAMELESS AND FACELESS
HE WHO STANDS GUARD –
PROTECTOR
CLOAKED IN MYSTERY

MOVERS AND SHAKERS SOUGHT TO CHANGE AND IMAGINE THE RHYTHM OF LIFE

ALONE IN THE DARK
CONTEMPLATING LIFE AND LOVE
SHADOWED BY THE BLUES

━━━━━━━━━━━━━━━━━━━━━━

PEOPLE YESTERDAY
SLUMBER STILL AND UNSPOKEN
COVERED BY THEIR DEEDS

━━━━━━━━━━━━━━━━━━━━━━

TIP-TOED, ON MY FEET
I WAVED AWAY YESTERDAY
TO DANCE UNTIL DAWN

17 Strokes: A Brushstroke of the Soul– Page 82

DRUMMER AND HIS KIDS GATHER TOGETHER TO PLAY A DIFFERENT TUNE

THE SEED OF LOVE GROWS WAITING TO BE BORN THE DAY MOTHERHOOD BEGINS

AT THE EDGE OF LOVE
WE CHANCED UPON A MEETING
NOT WILLING TO FALL

BATTLE WEARY MEN
SEE LIFE THROUGH BROKEN EYES
VOID OF EMOTION

--•--

IN DREAMS SHADOWS COME
WHILE WE WAIT TO CLIMB THE STAIRS
INTO THE KINGDOM

--•--

BRILLIANT COLORS
GLOW IN MOONLIGHT'S SERENADE
SOOTHE RAGING WATERS

—•—

TETHERED TO ANGELS
I DANCED NAKED ON THE STARS
UNTIL LIGHT OF DAY

—•—

KALEIDOSCOPIC
WHORLS OF COLORED MIST
LANDSCAPE OF MY MIND

A BURGUNDY MASK OF PRETENTIOUSNESS HIDES CRUELTY WITHIN

RECESSES OF SPACE,
INTER-DIMENSIONAL RIFTS
RIP THROUGH TIME'S FABRIC

IN THE DISMAL FIELDS
OF GREY COVERED ROCKY PATHS
NATURE FINDS A WAY

MIRRORED REFLECTIONS
EARTH AND SKY'S ABOUNDING LIGHT
FEEDING EACH OTHER

CAPTURED INNOCENCE
LOST TO LYING MEN IN WAIT
POWER HUNGRY CURS

GREED AT THE EXPENSE
OF THE LOST AND INNOCENT
LIVES LAID DOWN TO REST

NEWLY FORMED PETALS
AN EXQUISITE THRUST AT LIFE
BEAUTEOUS TO EYES

BLUE MAN LIVES WITHIN BOUNDARIES OF SPACE AND TIME TRANSCENDING MATTER

PAINT COLORED CANVAS
BROAD STROKES OF VIBRANT COLOR
INNER SPACE OF MIND

—•—•—•—•—•—•—•—•—•—•—•—•—•—•—•—•—•—•—•—

MEADOW'S DELIGHTFUL
SPLASH OF WHITE IN HEATHER FIELDS
A BREATH OF FRESH AIR

—•—•—•—•—•—•—•—•—•—•—•—•—•—•—•—•—•—•—•—

ELEMENTAL GIVE AND TAKE OF NATURES ROCKY CLIMB FROM WATER'S BASE

CONTRADICTORY
SIGHTS AND SOUNDS BLOW
HOT AND COLD
IN THE LIGHT OF DAY

—•—•—•—•—•—•—•—•—•—•—•—•—•—•—•—•—•—•—•—

MY SOUL FEELS THE BLUES
BOTH TURBULENT AND FIERY
DOWN DEEP IN MY HEART

—•—•—•—•—•—•—•—•—•—•—•—•—•—•—•—•—•—•—•—

ON CLOUDS BLUE AND WHITE
EMERGES A LIVING THING
TO SUSTAIN THE WORLD

SHIELDED BY THE WALL
I PEERED THROUGH NIGHT'S
SWEET EMBRACE
TO FIND EMPTINESS

DAWN OF A NEW DAY
CARRIES HOPE FOR BETTER THINGS
WE DARE TO DREAM OF

MAJESTIC BEAUTY
ON THE BANKS OF WINTER'S DAY
OVERSEE MANKIND

BURROWED IN THE EARTH
THE ROOTS OF WORLD'S
BREATH BEGAN
TO CLEAR THE FOUL AIR

TASTED OF THE FRUIT
IN A GARDEN LONG AGO
LOST CHASTITY

RAINBOW COLORED GLASS REFLECT LIFE'S MANY FACETS IN DIFFERENT HUES

WAITING FOR THE STORM
TEARDROPS FALL FROM UP ON HIGH
FROM HEAVEN'S OWN GATE

WATCH, WAIT AND SEE IS THE OBSERVER'S WAY TO BE WHICH CONSUMMATES ME

LUMINESCENT LIGHT
SCATTERING DARK BEFORE DAWN
REVEALS PATHS TO TAKE

————————————————————————————————

UP, UP AND AWAY
MY CARES JUST FLOATED AWAY
AS I ROSE ABOVE

————————————————————————————————

FLOWER POWER PEACE
MEETS A HARDENING OF HEARTS
WHERE LOVE WAITS TO LIVE

A BLURRED VISION
REFLECTED ON CALM WATERS
REMAINS UNDEFINED

LET THINGS OF THIS LIFE NEITHER TROUBLE NOR WEARY, BE THE WATERFALLS

CALM OR TURBULENT
BOTH WILL CONTINUE
OBSTACLES OR NOT

A CLASH OF COLORS
FIGHTING FOR SUPREMACY
OVER THE NEW DAY

HOW FAR WILL WE GO
TO SAVE A DYING PLANET
FROM MAN'S HUNGRY GREED

INTO SPACE WE SEEK
ANOTHER PLACE TO LIVE
AND BREATHE
FROM A WORLD DESTROYED

ON THE BANKS OF TIME
A PREDATOR WAITS NEARBY
UNSUSPECTINGLY

BEAUTEOUS VISTAS
AS FAR AS THE EYE CAN SEE
SATISFY OUR MINDS

ARE YOU KIDDING ME?
HIS EXPRESSION SEEMED TO SAY
ONE BRIGHT SUMMER'S DAY

FROM THE MIND OF MAN
A SHADOW OF FORMER SELF
WITHERS TO NOTHING

LAYER BY LAYER
FOUNDATIONS TO BUILD UPON
BRING BEAUTY TO LIFE

FALL HAS SET ASIDE
THE TIME FOR LEAVES TO DIE
FOR SPRING TO REBIRTH

SOMETIMES PERSPECTIVE
NEEDS TO BE READJUSTED
FOR A BALANCED MIND

TAKE A LEAP OF FAITH
INTO UNCHARTED WATERS
CHALLENGING THE NORM

FORTRESS LIES IN WAIT
PLUNDERED GOODS
ANDBODY COUNTS
FROM THE DESERT STORM

—•—•—•—•—•—•—•—•—•—•—•—•—•—•—•—

ADRIFT IN THE SNOW
CAUGHT IN NATURE'S
MIGHTY WRATH
WITH NO PLACE TO GO

—•—•—•—•—•—•—•—•—•—•—•—•—•—•—•—

BLOOMS OF PINK AND WHITE
BRIGHTEN UP A DREARY DAY
BY THE WINDOW SILL

MIGHTY POLAR BEAR
TRANSFORMS INTO
A DROWNED RAT
WHEN ARCTIC ICE MELTS

DEEP WITHIN MY HEART
THE MEMORY OF WHAT IF
REMAINS TO THIS DAY

─────────────────────────────

TROUBLES OF THE DAY FADE AWAY AS I SIT AND THINK UPON MY BLESSINGS

─────────────────────────────

RHYTHM AND THE BLUES
A FACT OF LIFE NOT DENIED
BROTHERS HAND IN HAND

WHEN VULNERABLE
IN THE WORLD OF PARADIGM
HIDDEN DIMENSIONS EXIST

BAD ART IMITATES
LIFE AMIDST ALL ITS FOIBLES
UNREMITTINGLY

—•—•—•—•—•—•—•—•—•—•—•—•—•—•—•—•—•—•—

RELIEF FROM THE DARK
OF JADED ROCK RECESSES
WATER STREAMS BELOW

—•—•—•—•—•—•—•—•—•—•—•—•—•—•—•—•—•—•—

FAMILY, A GIFT
OF LOVE IN A FIELD OF FIRE
TAMES BURNING EMBERS

CALM SERENITY,
WATER'S GIVE AND FLOW OF LIFE
COOLS HEAT'S INTENSITY

$$\cdot - \cdot - \cdot - \cdot - \cdot - \cdot - \cdot - \cdot - \cdot - \cdot - \cdot - \cdot - \cdot - \cdot - \cdot -$$

I LOOKED AND BEHELD
THE BEAUTY OF GOD'S CREATION
AND SAW IT WAS GOOD

$$\cdot - \cdot - \cdot - \cdot - \cdot - \cdot - \cdot - \cdot - \cdot - \cdot - \cdot - \cdot - \cdot - \cdot - \cdot -$$

ANIMALS REVEAL NURTURING IN MANY FORMS VOID OF VIOLENCE

SLANTED VIEWS OF LIFE
UNVARNISHED TRUTHS
AND QUESTIONS
ALWAYS BEING ASKED

LIGHT PIERCES HAZY NIGHTS BY THE SIDE OF THE LAKE WAITING FOR MORNING

—•—•—•—•—•—•—•—•—•—•—•—•—•—•—•—•—•—•—

WILD FLOWERS GROW RAMPANT UNCHECKED, UNTAMED AND FREELY IN WAYS SELDOM SEEN

—•—•—•—•—•—•—•—•—•—•—•—•—•—•—•—•—•—•—

NATURE'S GUARDIAN OVERSEES THE WAY WE LIVE ON THIS PALE BLUE DOT

SOAR FREELY OVER
THE SEA'S TEMPESTUOUS STORMS
TO FLY WILD AND FREE

IN SIMPLICITY
BEAUTY GROWS BY LEAPS AND BOUNDS
FROM A SINGLE SEED

THE EDGE OF THE WOODS
A NATURAL BARRIER
FROM PAST TO PRESENT

MOUNTAINS TO BE SCALED
A TRAJECTORY THROUGH LIFE
FROM BIRTH UNTIL DEATH

FIVE TO ON THE CLOCK
MINUTES FROM OUR DAILY LIVES
IT'S TIME TO DECIDE

CLOAKED IN PURPLE CLOTH
UNENCUMBERED BY THE PAST
A NEW FUTURE WAITS

SEA'S TIDES EBB AND FLOW
LIKE MAN'S VOLATILITY
WHEN WINDS BLOW FIERCELY

SEAS OF BLUES AND WHITES
UNFORGIVING STORMS ROAR FREE
TIME TO SWIM OR DROWN

CLIMB THE HIGHEST PEAKS
THEN LOOK AT HOW
FAR YOU'VE COME
ROCK BOTTOM TO TOP

— · — · — · — · — · — · — · — · — · — · — · — · — · —

UNCLIPPED WINGS FLY HIGH
RISE FROM A DISCONTENTED
MOTHER NATURE'S SPLEEN

— · — · — · — · — · — · — · — · — · — · — · — · — · —

A GRAIN OF SAND ROSE
TO GREAT AND TOWERING HEIGHTS
BUILT ROCK UPON ROCK

ECLECTIC COLORS
DANCE OVER ROCKY LANDSCAPES
THE DAY'S SETTING SUN

CHOOSE THE HIGHEST PATH
LESS TRAVELLED BY THE MANY
SELDOM SEEN BY FEW

LIFE'S FLUIDITY
ERODES EVEN THE HARSHEST
OF ENVIRONMENTS

BLUE SKIES DO INVITE
A DEEPER EXPLORATION
OF NATURE'S BOUNTY

---·---

BACKWARDS AND FORWARDS
I BEND TO ALLOW FOR CHANGE
FROM WHAT I ONCE WAS

---·---

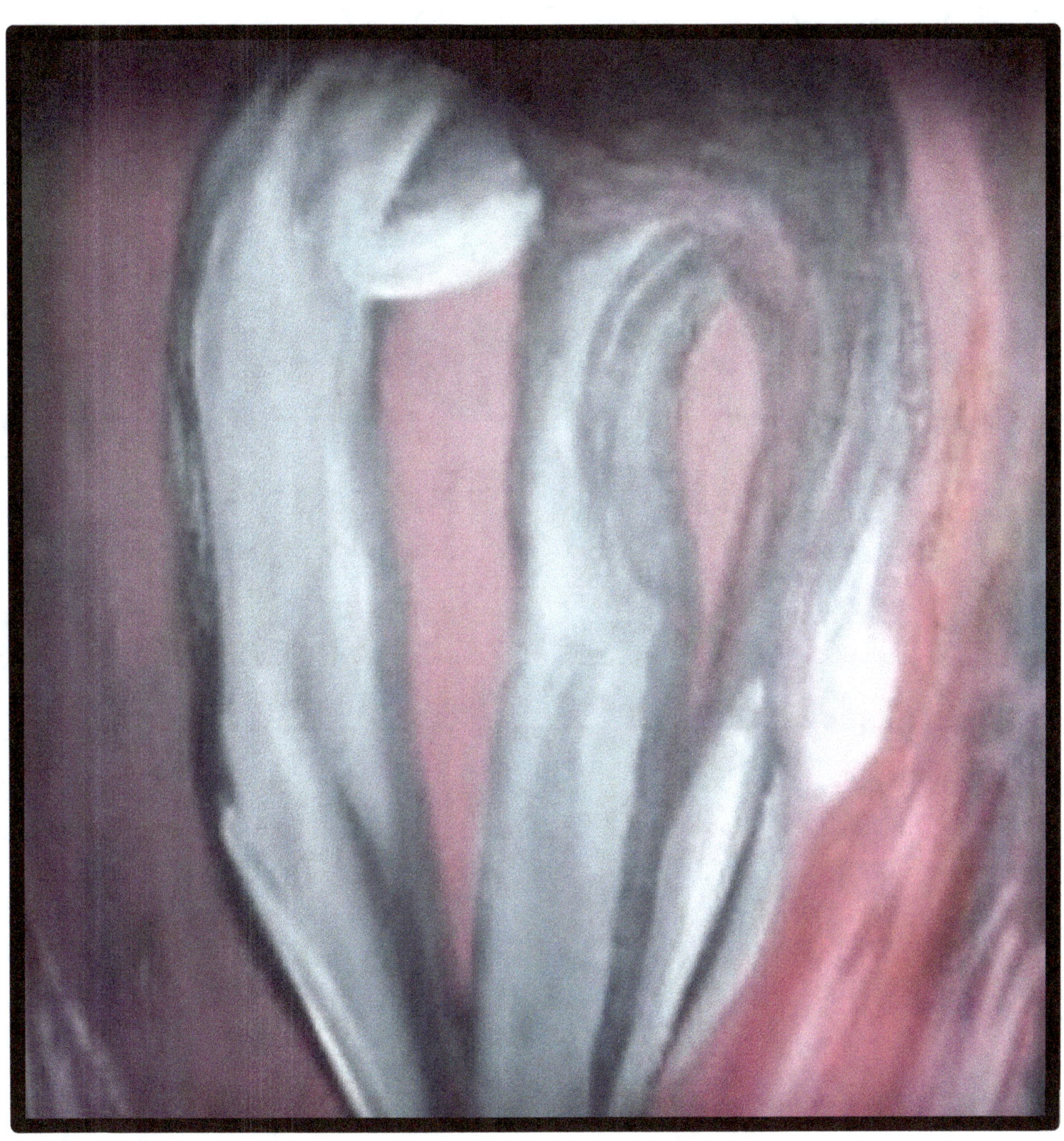

THE LEFT OR THE RIGHT
ONE EXTREME OR THE OTHER
WITH NO MIDDLE GROUND

EVEN UPHILL CLIMBS
REVEAL AN INNER BEAUTY
STRENGTH AND ENDURANCE

DRESSED LIKE SANTA CLAUS
ON A COLD, WINTERY DAY
NEW LIFE WAITS TO BIRTH

TAKE A LOOK AND SEE
AN EXQUISITE TAPESTRY
REVEALED TO OUR EYES

FROM THE HAND OF GOD
WE'RE INVITED TO PARTAKE
OF HIS GIFT TO US

IGNORANT OF LOVE
WE SACRIFICE INNOCENCE
FOR GREED AND POWER

SELF-IDENTITY
MEASURED BY THE BODY'S SKIN
TO BE PREYED UPON

NEW EXPERIMENTS REVEAL POSSIBILITIES ON A BLANK CANVAS

INROADS COME AND GO
AND THE WORK BEGINS AGAIN
CREATIVITY

TILT YOUR HEAD THIS WAY
AND YOUR PERCEPTION
WILL CHANGE
TO SEE SOMETHING NEW

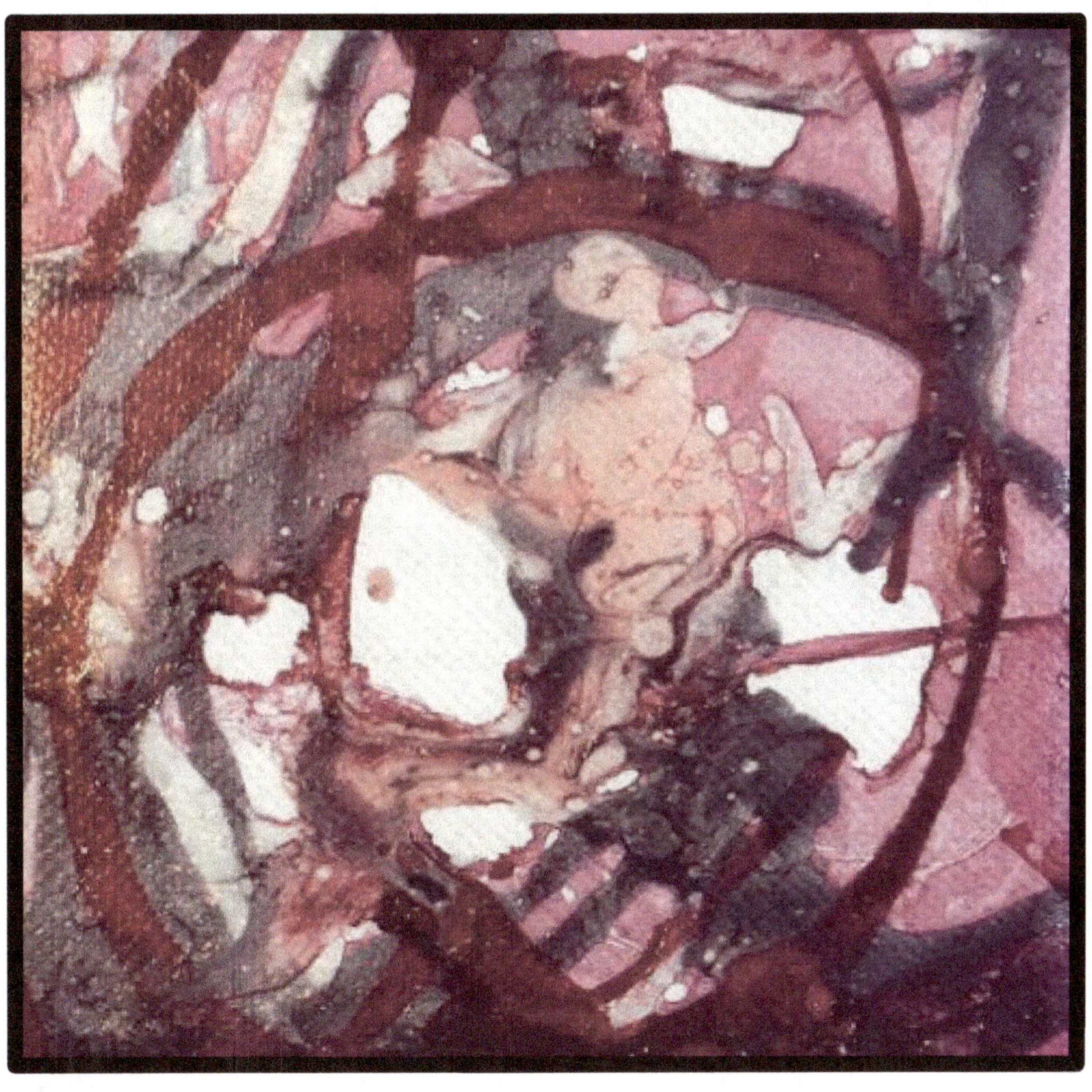

—·—

RANDOM VEINS OF GOLD
TRAVEL THROUGH
THE UNDERWORLD
NATURE'S MOTHER LOAD

—·—

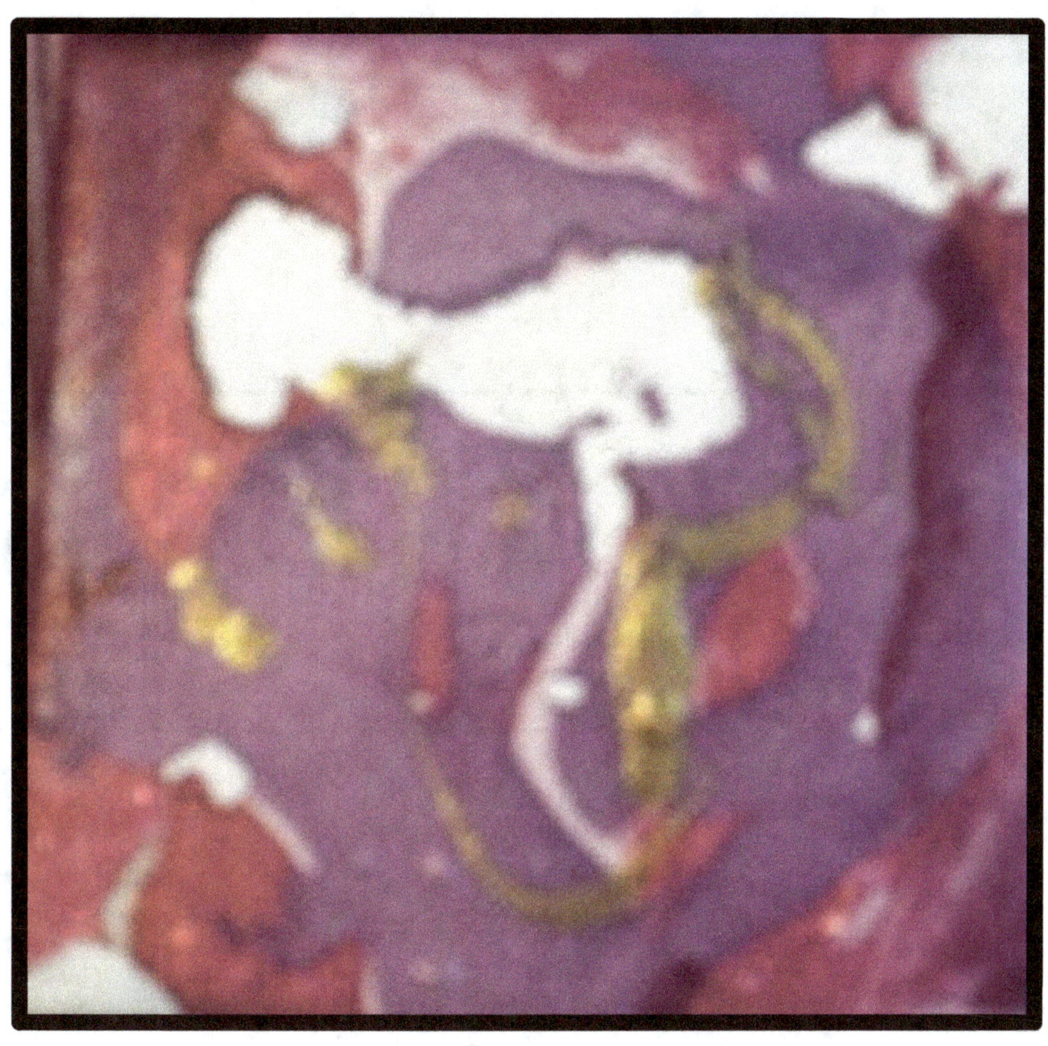

BUBBLES OF AIR RISE
TO BREAK THE STAGNANT WATER
BREATHING LIFE INSIDE

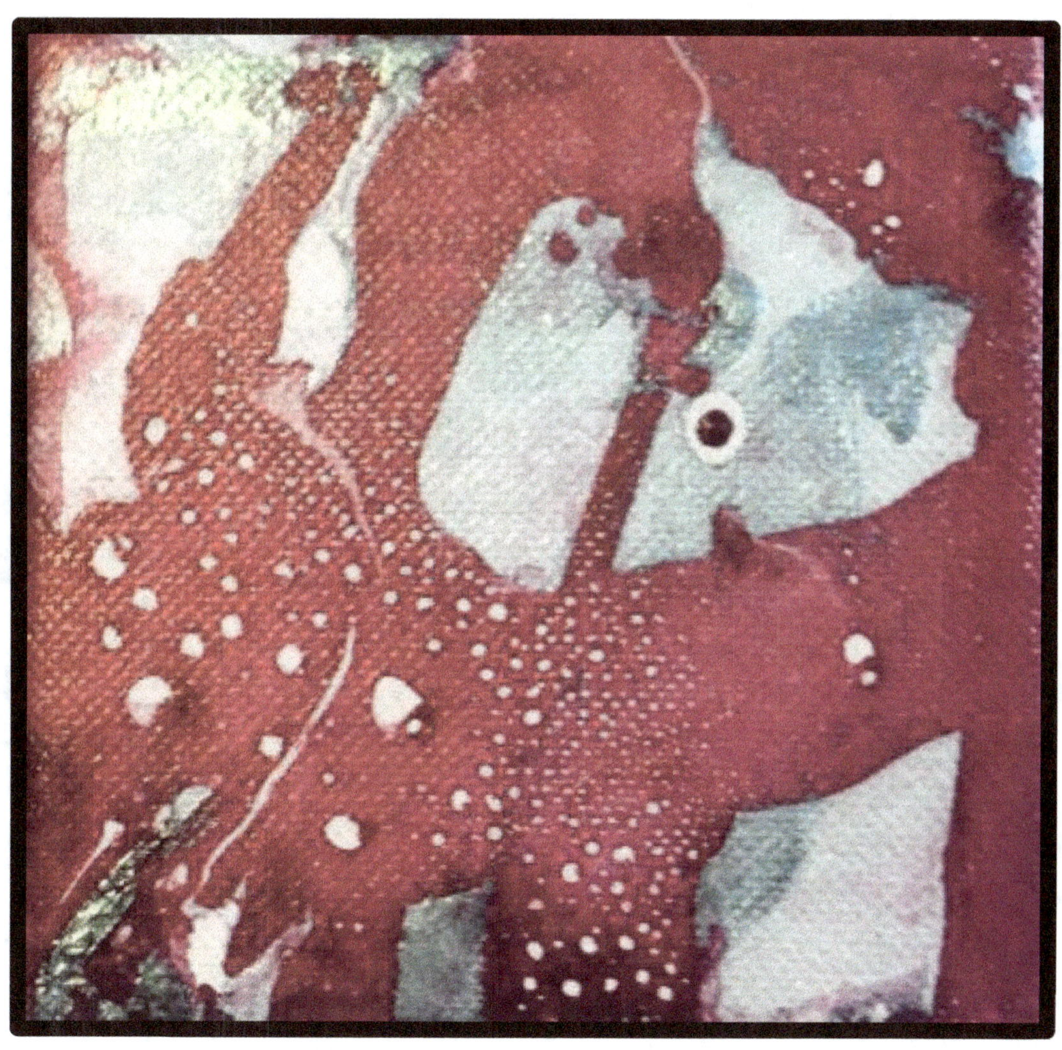

STRINGS STRUNG TOGETHER
LIKE THE CHORDS ON A GUITAR
CREATING MUSIC

A TIE CAST ASIDE, SUPERFLUOUS, UNWANTED CASUAL TODAY

I WILL BEND BEFORE
THE BOUGH BREAKS,
TO STAND AHEAD
OF THE PACK ALONE

A SEEDLING GROWS TALL
FIRMLY PLANTED IN THE SOIL
TO BE UPROOTED

—•—

CHRISTMAS GREENS AND GOLD
BRING FORTH THE
GREATEST PLEASURES
TO BOTH, YOUNG AND OLD

—•—

BROKEN WINDOWPANES
STILL REVEAL BOTH NIGHT AND DAY
INSIDE AND OUTSIDE

— • — • — • — • — • — • — • — • — • — • — • — • — • — • —

CONFINES OF THE CAGE
MAKES THINKING OUTSIDE THE BOX
DIFFICULT AS HELL

— • — • — • — • — • — • — • — • — • — • — • — • — • —

TUCKED SAFELY BEHIND
A MESH WIRED GILDED CAGE
FREEDOM IS WITHHELD

———————————————————————————

THE WORLD KEEPS TURNING DESPITE WHAT MAY BEFALL IT, AND LIFE WILL STILL GROW

———————————————————————————

HONEY-MAKING BEES
BIRDS SOAR LOFTY COLORED SKIES
THE POND REMAINS STILL

LIFE, ADRIFT LIKE ME,
WATCHING SAFELY ASHORE
WHICH WAY THE WINDS BLEW

SUN KISSED RAYS OF LIGHT
A BRILLIANT SHIMMERY
SURFACE TO PONDER

—•—•—•—•—•—•—•—•—•—•—•—•—•—•—•—•—•—•—

BIRDS BASK IN SUN'S LIGHT
SETTING AT THE END OF DAY
HEADING FOR ITS NEST

—•—•—•—•—•—•—•—•—•—•—•—•—•—•—•—•—•—•—

———————————————

FROM THE HIGHEST PEAK
I PEERED INTO THE ABYSS
THAT I OVERCAME

———————————————

VARIED DIMENSIONS OBSTRUCTIONS UPON THE PATH MEANT TO CIRCUMVENT

A DIFFERENT WAY
PRESENTS ITSELF FOR THE CLIMB
FROM ROCK BOTTOM UP

DIMENSIONAL RIFT
IN SPACE TIME CONTINUUM
POSSIBILITIES

HAND UPON MY HEART
MEMORIES RESURRECTED
LIVE ANOTHER DAY

———————————————

THE SUN OF MY HEART
REMAINS WITHIN MY LOCKET
WORN EVERY DAY

———————————————

IN THE LAND OF GEEK
THE NERD IS THE MUSICIAN
A BARD STRUMMING CODE

$$-\cdot-\cdot-\cdot-\cdot-\cdot-\cdot-\cdot-\cdot-\cdot-\cdot-\cdot-\cdot-$$

IN MANY FORMS DOES SPLENDOR COME TO BRIGHTEN UP A DULL, DREARY DAY!

$$-\cdot-\cdot-\cdot-\cdot-\cdot-\cdot-\cdot-\cdot-\cdot-\cdot-\cdot-\cdot-$$

THE PAINTER NEEDS TO GO WITHIN TO FIND THE MUSE FOR PERSPECTIVE'S SAKE!

—•—•—•—•—•—•—•—•—•—•—•—•—•—•—•—•—

TWO HEARTS COLLIDED
TIME'S GONE BY, PAST AND PRESENT
FUTURE'S YET TO COME

—•—•—•—•—•—•—•—•—•—•—•—•—•—•—•—•—

TANGLED PATTERNS WEAVE
TO CREATE PURE ABSTRACTION
INCANDESCENT THOUGHTS

REMNANTS OF MORTAR
REST UPON THE SHORES OF LIFE
ONCE WITHIN ITS WALLS

PATTERNS BLEED AND MERGE
BOUND TOGETHER SIDE BY SIDE
OVERLAPPING LINES

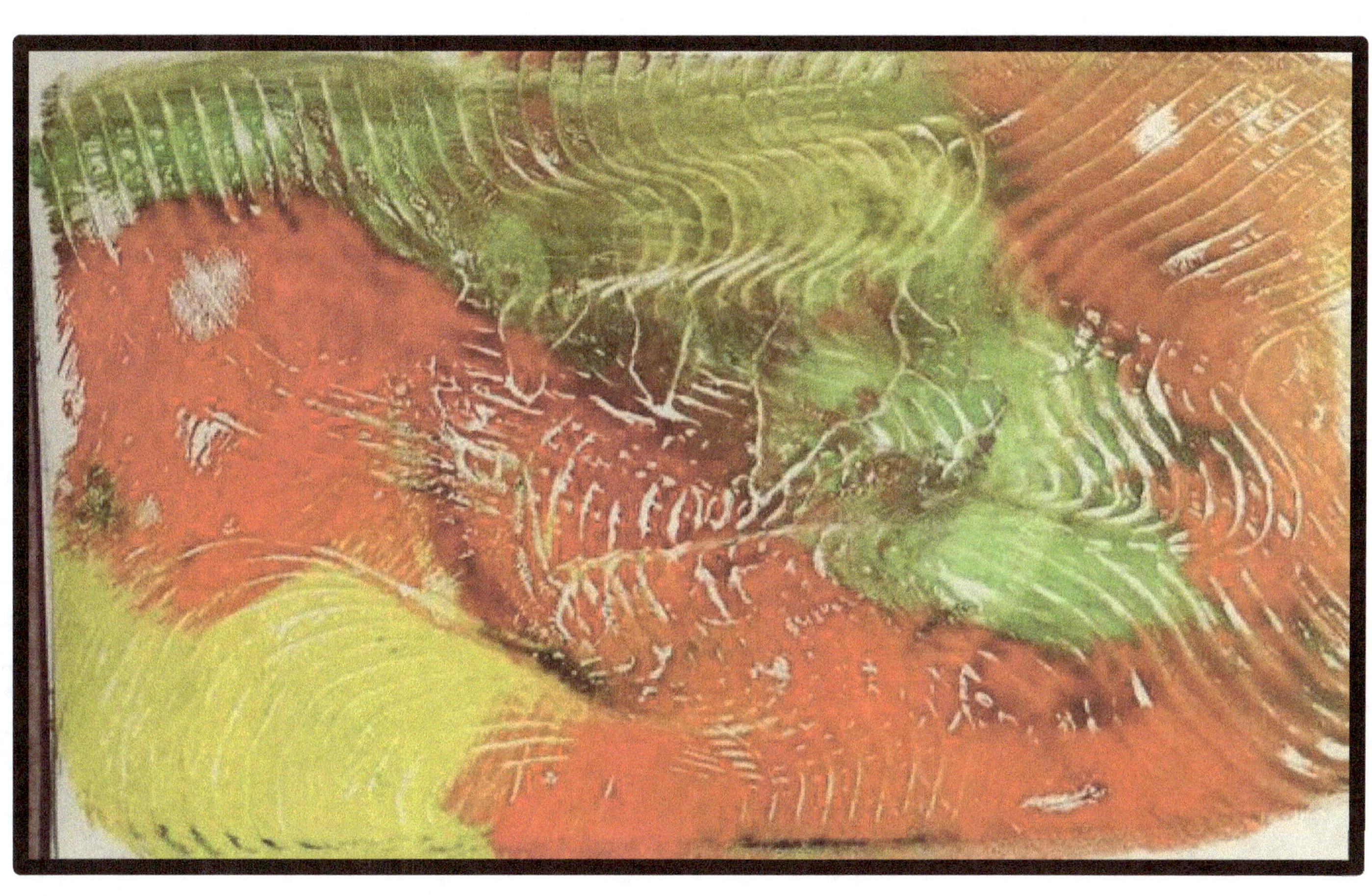

THE HINT OF DARKNESS
SEEKS TO BLOT OUT LIGHT OF DAY
UP AND DOWN THE GRID

THEY CROSSED THE THRESHOLD TO ANOTHER DIMENSION AVERTING DANGER

REAMS OF BOLD COLOR
FILL THE PAGE FROM LEFT TO RIGHT
AN ECLECTIC SIGHT

LIGHTNESS OF BEING PROVIDING HELPING HANDS WITHOUT RECOMPENSE

SQUIGGLED COLOURED LINES CROSSING AND INTERSECTING FORM RANDOM PATTERNS

SHIELDED FROM THE WORLD
A FAMILY IN NATURE
WALK THEIR QUIET PATH

MOVEMENT TO AND FRO
A CLASH OF TEMPERAMENTS
PERMEATE THE SPACE

HUMBLE AND GENTLE
HIS WORD ENDURES FOREVER
HE TAUGHT US TO LOVE

HID WITHIN EACH MAN
THE TRUE FACE OF SELF IS MASKED
WILL TRUTH COME TO LIGHT?

MELTING POLAR CAPS
WHERE BEARS SEEK
TO FIND NEW GROUND
EVERMORE DISTANT

DAISY CHAINS AND CROWNS
EACH PETAL TELLS A STORY
'TIL THE LAST ONE'S GONE

TOPSY TURVY STROKES
LIKE THE WORLD IN WHICH WE LIVE
ALL IS UPSIDE DOWN

WINDBLOWN STEMS AND TWIGS HALF-DEAD FLOWERS STILL LIVE ON IN AN ARTIST'S WORLD

EYES TELL A STORY
OFTEN UNREAD BY OTHERS
AND SELDOM EXPRESSED

—•—

JUST LIKE THINGS IN LIFE
SLANTED VIEWS
AND ARGUMENTS
WAITING FOR THE YIELD

—•—•—•—•—•—•—•—•—•—•—•—•—•—•—•—•—•—•—•—

•—•—•—•—•—•—•—•—•—•—•—•—•—•—•—•—•—•

SILENCE UNDISTURBED
ON A CRISP, COLD WINTER'S DAY
WAITING FOR LAUGHTER

•—•—•—•—•—•—•—•—•—•—•—•—•—•—•—•—•—•

LIGHT CASTS A SHADOW
LIKE THAT OF HUMAN PSYCHE
WHICH IS DARK OR BRIGHT?

SNOWMAN WAITS IN VAIN
FOR THE SNOWBALL FIGHT TO START
WHERE ARE THE CHILDREN?

———————————————————————

SOMETIMES WE MAKE WAVES THAT DON'T SIT WELL WITH OTHERS AND THE CURRENTS CHANGE

———————————————————————

- -

THE SUN WAITS TO RISE
WHILE THE DARKNESS FADES AWAY
GIVING WAY TO DAY

- -

—•—•—•—•—•—•—•—•—•—•—•—•—•—•—•—•—•—

ARTIST AND WRITER
I'M DEBORAH MCINTOSH
WELCOME TO MY MIND!

—•—•—•—•—•—•—•—•—•—•—•—•—•—•—•—•—•—